More from My
Heart

A COLLECTION OF POEMS

Randolph Baltimore

Print information available on the last page

Rev. date: 07/28/2015

To order additional copies of this book, contact:
Xlibris
1-888-795-4274
www.Xlibris.com
Orders@Xlibris.com

Table of Contents

I often sit and think about how nice it would be to one day cross the threshold and find that someone you've long been waiting for.

Open the Door

—❧—

Some day I'd love to open the door
Find you standing there
Knowing that you care
Love filling the air.

Some day I'd love to open the door
Find you on the other side
With arms open wide
Someone in whom to confide.

Some day I'd love to open the door
Find a faithful friend
On whom I can depend
Whose love has no end.

But for me these things are a fantasy.

Hope some day they will become reality.

Guess I'll just have to wait and see

What fate has in store for me.

Some day I'd love to open the door

Find a loving Dad

Run and sit in his lap.

Something I've never had.

Some day I'd love to open the door

Find a loving mother

With so much love it would smother me,

My sisters and brothers.

But for me these things are just a dream.

Hope one day they'll come to be

Manifest in my life tangibly.

Maybe it's in the works behind the scenes.

So often the door has been slammed in my face

'Til I've felt like forfeiting this life's race.

So often the door has kicked me in the heart

'Til I've felt like from this life I'll depart.

But somewhere deep inside I have hope

That whatever life brings my way I will cope.

And somewhere deep inside I have faith

That things won't always be this way.

Some day I'd love to open the door

And from my face tears will flow

As I gaze upon what's me before

Everything my heart's been longing for.

On May 10, 2008, I lost my beautiful niece, Dawn Michelle Allen. She was born with her heart on the right side, a very rare case. The doctors said she wouldn't live for six months but we were blessed to have her for 34 years. On her last day as we gathered around her bedside, although she had been heavily sedated, right before she took her last breath she opened her eyes and smiled. I wrote this poem for Dawn's mother, my sister, Youdella.

Dawn

I will always treasure that first wintry morn
After the night on which you were born
When I gently cradled you in my arms
And smiled at you my newborn, Dawn.

Wrinkled with a reddish tint to your skin
I loved you from without and within.
So gladly were you welcomed into the world,
My first-born, precious little girl.

Unlimited joy you brought to so many.
Unconditional love, you had plenty.
Purity in you was personified.
The love of Jesus shined in your eyes.

Though your first few years had a rocky start

From complications of the heart

On you I never, ever gave up.

Oh, there's just nothing like a mother's love!

A long, hard road with you I traveled.

At times I felt like coming unraveled.

But with perseverance and strong faith,

I faced each difficult and trying day.

Up ahead there was a fork in the road.

Should I go left or right? I needed to know.

Were you to go or were you to stay?

But with the outcome God had the final say.

Looking back I have no regrets
Of the tough decisions with which I was met.
You're at peace now with the One who created you
And I await the day when I can be with you too.

Though physically you're not here for a reason,
I realize you were on loan to me for a season.
Your purpose here many didn't understand
But I know for sure it was the Master's plan.

I will always treasure that first wintry morn
After the night on which you were born.
I await to cradle you once again in my arms
And smile at you on that New Day, Dawn.

Human

---·❦·---

I don't always cross every 'T' and dot every 'I'.
Sometimes I might tell a little white lie.
But one thing's for sure that can't be denied,
That's what it is to be human.

I don't always take time to say grace.
Sometimes I end up with egg on my face.
But one thing's for sure that can't be erased,
That's what it is to be human.

I don't always hit the mark.
Sometimes I don't even hit the ball out of the park.
But one thing's for sure that can't be chalked,
That's what it is to be human.

From the time I awake until I close my eyes,

From the moment I'm born until the day I die,

Until the angels come and take me to the sky,

I am H – U – M – A – N – I – T – Y.

I don't always get up when down I fall.

Sometimes I do things that might you appall.

But one thing's for sure that can't be recalled,

That's what it is to be human.

I don't always do what is right.

Sometimes I might tell you to go take a flight.

But one thing's for sure that you cannot fight,

That's what it is to be human.

I don't always say 'Please' or 'Thank you, Ma'am'.

Sometimes I just don't give a damn.

But one thing's for sure that can't be slammed,

That's what it is to be human.

I am human and I make plenty of mistakes.

Sometimes to the point that my very soul quakes.

But in spite of what's in my life's outtakes,

Someone's there for me who never forsakes.

I don't always dot every 'I' and cross every 'T'.

Sometimes I break down and when cut I will bleed.

But one thing's for sure and please take heed,

That's what it is to be human.

From the time I awake until I close my eyes,

From the moment I'm born until the day I die,

Until the angels come and take me to the sky,

I am H – U – M – A – N – I – T – Y.

From the rising of the sun until it sets again,

From the beginning of spring until the winter's end,

Until I'm totally set free from sin,

I am H – U – M – A – N, my friend.

True Definition

---❦---

I look in the mirror
Roll up my sleeves
Flex the muscles a little
Kind of like what I see.
Been working out
Not for fame or recognition.
Just trying to stay in shape and get some definition.

But there's more to me than just the physical.
I have emotions, a soul, the inner man, the spiritual.
Bodily exercise profits to some degree
But what is most important lasts eternally.

Designer clothes, fancy cars,

A 401K, a prestigious job.

A large bank account, a skyrocketing career yet.

A case of Krystal, a baby blue Lear jet.

The wall in the den filled with various degrees.

A 42-inch flat screen HDTV.

All these things are nice but not everlasting.

What one truly needs these things are masking.

Some people think these things define you

But the reality is they only blind you.

Some people think these things constitute your worth

But they only disintegrate and return to the earth.

There's nothing wrong with having material possessions

But be a good steward and use some discretion.

Take care of those around you, the poor and the needy.

Don't hoard what you have becoming selfish and greedy.

God wants to transform you in the inner man.

He wants to direct and unfold your life's plan.

And when this happens you're going to see

A change outwardly as well as inwardly.

I look in the mirror again

Roll up my sleeves

Flex the muscles a little,

Now something different I see.

No longer in need of material things for recognition.

I've been recreated.

Now that's true definition!

One day I saw an old lady walking down the street. She wasn't dressed very well, hair was mussed and she seemed kind of disoriented. My first impression was she was homeless or a bag lady. Part of me said, 'How did she end up like this?' Was it her fault? Was it society's? I don't know but as I passed by her I heard the word 'unblinded' in my mind and as I started writing this poem, I began to realize I was looking in a mirror when I was looking at her.

Unblinded

—— ❧ ——

Pointed my finger at you.

Said of you I have no use.

Was not aware of my abuse.

Tore you apart with my tongue.

Out to dry I wished you were hung.

Was not aware of how you I shunned.

Hurriedly covered up my nose

From your bodily stench that arose.

Was not aware of my own.

Passed you by many times on the street.

Noticed your tired and aching feet.

Was totally aware I didn't speak.

Closed my hands when near you came

With a growling stomach you needed tamed.

Didn't care to know your name.

But one day on me the tables turned.

Lost everything I ever earned.

Never dreamed I would ever be burned.

Rapidly I fell to the ground.

Everything vanished — no one around.

The silence became a frightening sound.

Looked up and saw you standing there.
Freed from all your pain and despair,
Reaching out to me with loving care.

You pulled me from the ditch I had dug.
Cleansed me, clothed me, kissed me and hugged.
Never once did me you judge.

Placed me on the rightful path,
Straight ahead not looking back.
"Do unto others" is all you asked.

Set me free of being proud-minded.
My past forgiven. Don't want to rewind it.
Just so grateful to be unblinded.

I was recently thinking about the life of a pioneer; how he blazes trails, risks his life making new discoveries that will benefit mankind. Although the outcome of what he does is great and everlasting I've often wondered about the road it takes to get there and what goes through his mind.

Come By

Can you come by and see me?

Can you come by today?

Can you come by and see me

Maybe for a little while and stay?

Been travelling a lonely road

And need a little company.

Been travelling a lonely road

And need what you bring to me.

Can you come by and see me?

Can you come by today?

Can you come by and see me

Maybe for a little while to stay?

Been travelling a lonely road.

Seems like forever I've tarried.

Been shouldering a heavy load

And need some help to carry.

Life has a lot of twists and turns.

Kind of hard to figure out.

Life has a lot of bruises and burns

And is full of hopes and doubts.

Some things we know in part.

Maybe that's how it's supposed to be.

Some things end so others can start.

Maybe that's how it's supposed to be.

So can you come by and see me

Maybe for an hour or two?

Can you come by and see me?

Then continue on with what you do.

Can you come by this morning

If you have a little time?

Can you stay until dawning

And help me ease my mind?

Need a shoulder to lean on
Someone in whom to confide.
Need a shoulder to lean on
And a bosom in which to hide.

You don't have to speak a word.
A touch is all I need.
It transcends what is heard
And does the job sufficiently.

Be my companion for a little while.
I know you will have to depart.
But at least we can have some quality time
To share what's on our hearts.

So can you come by and see me?
Can you come when time allows?
I'll be forever grateful to you my friend.
Forever grateful, this I vow.

A few years ago my dear friend, Darcey, invited me to a surprise birthday party for her husband, Jonas. A few days before the party I realized I hadn't bought him a card. I had only known him a short period of time and I didn't want to get him just any old card so I decided to go inside myself and create a card for him.

Jonas

Today on September twenty eighth
The time has come to celebrate
The birthday of a wonderful man
Not here by mistake but born as God planned.

From childhood and throughout your adult years
You overcame many doubts and fears,
Transformed into a strong and mighty man.
Not here by mistake but just as God planned.

Your name in Hebrew means the Dove
So appropriate, fits you like a hand in a glove.
So gentle and peaceful your personality.
So gracious and full of humility.

You're a father, a brother, husband and friend
Who is loved from without and loved from within.
There is so much to say, so much more to be told
About the man who's worth his weight in gold.

So I am honored to partake and celebrate
On today, September twenty-eighth,
The birthday of a wonderful man
Not here by mistake but born as God planned.

Transition

————— ❧ —————

How do I begin to comprehend what you are going through?

And how do I begin to understand when I hear about your news?

But I feel your pain because I have been placed in the same position

Having lost someone so close to me who has made the transition.

I know I can't try or even imply that I know what you're going through.

I know that I cry and sympathize when I hear about your news.

But I relate to your pain because I have been placed in the same positon

Having lost someone so close to me who has made the transition.

Life is short so the people say.

For many this truth has been slanted.

Tomorrow's not promised to anyone.

The present is what we've been granted.

We're pilgrims and strangers here on this earth.

Make the best as you're passing through.

A better life awaits those who believe,

A better life for me and you.

So what can I do to help you through this time of difficulty?

And what can I say to ease the pain of this catastrophe?

My hearts breaks for you as you're going through this time of intermission.

Having lost someone so close to you who has made the transition.

Love Again

—— ❦ ——

I remember the day I met you.
I didn't even know your name.
But somehow I knew deep down inside
That we were both the same.

I didn't know if I could talk to you.
I didn't even know what to say.
I've always been so painfully shy
So I turned and walked away.

But then you spoke
My heart awoke
And something changed inside.
My defenses came down,
Tumbled to the ground
When I looked into your eyes.

I saw hope again.

I saw love again

And I knew right then

I had found a true friend.

I don't know where this is going.

I don't even have a clue.

I'll just cherish each and every moment

That I'm sharing here with you.

I believe that we were meant to be.

I believe God has brought us together.

I believe that this is a true love,

A true love that will last forever.

And when you spoke

My heart awoke

And something changed inside.

My defenses came down

Tumbled down to the ground

When I looked in your eyes.

I saw hope again

I saw love again and I found a friend.

Hope this never ends.

I'm in love again.

I've been born again.

May this never end with you my friend.

Love was right around the corner

Waiting for me in the wings.

Love was right around the corner

Now my heart so gratefully sings.

Love was right around the corner

Wrapped up as you in disguise.

Love was right around the corner

And took me by surprise.

And when you spoke
My heart awoke
And something changed inside.

My defenses came down
Tumbled down to the ground
When I looked in your eyes.

I saw hope again.
I saw love again and I found a friend.
Hope this never ends.

I'm in love again.
I've been born again.
May this never end with you my friend.

Close the Door

—— ❧ ——

It started out as a little spark.
Turned into flames when you captured my heart.
With so much love into me you poured,
I don't ever want to close the door.

We started out just as friends.
Realized it would last until the end.
With so much love, who could ask for more?
I don't ever want to close the door.

Worked real hard and sacrificed.
This relationship we have is highly prized.
With so much love that overflows,
I don't ever want to close the door.

It's not perfect by any means.

Not like what's portrayed on the movie screen.

This is solid and real, beyond that and more.

I don't ever want to close the door.

Along the way we've had ups and downs

But faith and forgiveness turned things around.

There was no need for us to settle a score.

There was no need for us to ever close the door.

All my life I've waited for this love.

It's the kind that I have always dreamed of.

Pure and gentle, unconditional

Easily entreated and unconventional.

All my life I've waited for this love.

Delivered from heaven on the wings of a dove.

Pure, uplifting and energizing

Precious, priceless and uncompromising.

Oh, we've had our share of arguments and fights
But things were resolved before the fall of night.
With love dwelling at center of our core
We never worried about closing the door.

Unexpectedly came a wedge in between.
Tried to blow us to smithereens.
But we caught it in time before we were floored.
Thank God we were able to close the door!

All my life I've waited for this love.
It's the kind I've always dreamed of.
All my life I've waited for this love.
Fits perfectly like a hand in a glove.

We're in this till death do we part
Joined and fitted together at the heart.
With love flowing endless like the sands on the shore,
We will never, ever close the door.